THE MOUNTAIN MAN'S VALENTINE

A CURVY WOMAN STEAMY SHORT ROMANCE

ABBY GRAYLOVE

CONTENTS

1
______

CHRIS

"FIND THAT VALENTINE OF YOURS AND GIVE THEM A squeeze! This next one is for all of you lovebirds out there," the DJ croons over the radio. The wheedling opening notes of a sappy song strain through my truck's speakers.

I snap off the radio. Valentine's Day stuff never appealed to me—it all seems so artificial. But then, so does love. I've got real-world things to think about. Like the blizzard heading my way.

The weather is always a bear this time of year in Pine River, and this weekend looks to be no different. I'm heading into town to pick up supplies for the weekend. Depending on how bad the storm gets, it could be a few days before I can go anywhere.

"Chris, it's good to see you." Dale, a portly man in his fifties, extends a hand to me. He's one of my customers. I smile and shake his hand.

"Likewise. How's that picnic table been treating you?" I ask.

"Not much use for it in this weather," Dale laughs. "But we'll put it through its paces come springtime."

"Glad to hear it," I say. "Hey, I'm glad I ran into you. I wanted to ask you about that dining set I'm making for you right now."

"No trouble getting that mahogany, was there?" Dale asks.

"No, no, nothing like that. There's actually a competition coming up next month, right before your delivery date, and I think the dining set would be a perfect entry. It'd delay delivery by an extra week, but if you don't mind I'd like to enter the set before I bring it over to you."

"Competition, hmm? A chance to have another award-winning Chris Walker original gracing my chalet?" Dale is grinning. I smile and shrug. He's going to say yes.

"Assuming I win," I say. But Dale laughs.

"You'll win, Chris. Your work is the best thing this side of the Mississippi." He holds out his hand. "Yes, I'd love it if you enter it. The missus and I will do just fine with one more week of eating in the kitchen."

I've seen Dale's kitchen. Trust me when I say they will indeed be just fine.

"Sounds great," I say. "I'll shoot you an email with the details, and I'll be sure to let you know what medals I win." I don't like to count my chickens before they hatch, but I do think I've got a good shot in that competition. And Dale likes bragging to his friends—which brings me more business.

Dale and I say our goodbyes, and I make my way through the aisles, gathering my groceries.

"Mr. Chris, Mr. Chris!" A small voice shouts. I turn and see a small, dark-haired boy sprinting down the aisle towards me.

"Hey, Liam," I say. I bend down to be on his level. At

six feet and change, I tower over most people—and between my height, my beard, and the muscles I've built with my carpentry work, adults tend to find me intimidating. Kids, on the other hand, have no such qualms.

"Mr. Chris, do you have anything for me?" he asks. His mother appears behind him and chides him for his rudeness, but I laugh. I reach into my pocket.

"In fact I do," I tell him. I hold out a tiny bear, carved from walnut, about the size of my thumb. Liam's eyes grow bright with excitement.

"Wow," he says, "that is so cool. A bear! Roar!"

"It's yours," I tell him, giving the little carving to him. I host field trips from the local elementary school, so a lot of the kids in town get to know me and my work. Whenever I'm heading in to run errands, I try to remember to bring a few little carvings with me to distribute. The joy in their eyes makes it worth it.

His mother smiles at me in thanks. "You just made his week," she says.

"My pleasure," I say, standing and ruffling Liam's hair. He is making the toy bear crawl around and growl, his imagination turning the grocery aisle into the wild outdoors in an instant. "Have fun, buddy," I tell him.

"Thanks, Mr. Chris!" Liam exclaims, before resuming his game of pretend.

After I finish my shopping and check out, I step outside to see that the snow has already begun to fall. For now, it frosts the tops of cars and the tips of tree branches, but soon it will blanket the world in a heavy layer of white.

As I load my groceries into my truck, I think of the smile on Liam's face. I spent so much of my own childhood terrified and sad. Getting a chance to bring a little light into a kid's life is makes me feel like maybe my own life is worth something.

I'll never have kids of my own. After the way my parents fought—over me, around me, and right through me like I was invisible—right up until my dad drank himself to death, I know that I can't risk letting that pattern repeat itself. But hosting field trips, apprenticing older kids who are interested in carpentry—all of it gives me a chance to make their worlds a little brighter. It's my way of putting something good back out into the world.

PINE RIVER IS CLOSING UP, battening down the hatches and preparing for the incoming storm. I drive down Main Street, then make a right onto Spruce Street. The library stands out in the snow, its stone gable lit up like a stalwart bastion against the falling dusk.

I could stop in, I tell myself. Pick up something to watch or read to pass the weekend stuck inside.

It doesn't hurt that Olivia St. James works at the Pine Ridge library. Olivia is whip-smart and sharp-witted—just my type, if I let myself have one. She's gorgeous, too—curvy in all the right places, blonde hair, and a smile that outshines the sun.

Alright, so I have a little crush on Olivia. Not that I get crushes—at thirty-five, I'm way too old for that. And I'm not looking for a relationship either, now or ever. But if I were, Olivia would be exactly my type.

I pull my truck into the parking lot, parking next to a shiny silver Honda SUV. It stands out, since most of the cars around here have their usual winter coating of snow, ice, and salt, and it has only the first frosting of the falling snow.

I turn off the engine of my truck and take a deep breath. There's no reason to get nervous. It's just a trip to the library.

2

____

OLIVIA

"Thanks for your patronage! Enjoy your books," I say, smiling as I hand Mrs. Pryce her stack of novels. Romances and mysteries—exactly the way that I'd like to be spending my own weekend. But I have other plans.

"So, tell me more about this event you're going to," Ellie says, scooting her chair over closer to mine. A few people are still browsing around the library, picking up their last items before we close tonight. As usual, Friday night is a bit of a rush. Even more so with the incoming snow. But there's a lull in patrons at the circulation desk, and Ellie capitalizes on the opportunity to corner me about my love life—or lack thereof.

I sigh. "It's a Valentine's Day singles mixer event," I say, keeping my voice low. "It's in the city, at one of the big hotels." The event is scheduled for Friday night, tonight, with an option to make a dinner reservation for Valentine's Day on Sunday if you hit it off with anyone.

I had signed up on a whim, desperate to avoid spending yet another v-word day alone.

"Ooo, so you're having like a little weekend getaway? I'm so jealous," Ellie says. I hide my eye roll.

"Should be fun," I lie. The truth is, I'm not looking forward to going. I'm only in my early thirties, but I feel like I'm running out of time to have a life. It feels like my clock is ticking on finding someone to fall in love with, someone to marry and have kids with, and this dating event is just like tossing a thimble of water onto a house fire. I tell myself that I have to try, that I have to put myself out there if I want to find love. But everyone I know who is married met their spouse in college. My college boyfriend cheated on me—repeatedly.

I suppose there are worse things than being single. I could have ended up married to Chad.

Still, I feel a little guilty about leaving Simon—my cat—alone for the weekend. I had set up his food timer and litter box before I left for work. I'm headed straight to the event as soon as the library closes—and I'll have to hope I don't hit traffic if I want to avoid being late.

The weather wasn't part of my plan. But I'm not going to let a little snow stop me.

"You look cute," Ellie says. "I like your skirt."

I thank her and glance down at my outfit. I've chosen a bright red pleated skirt and a cream-colored sweater that hugs me in all the right places. It's a little showier than I would normally go for, but I like the way it looks on me. I toy with my necklace and try not to think too much about everything that could go wrong at the event.

"If I'm going to make it to the mixer tonight I'll have to head out as soon as we close," I tell Ellie. I've told her three times already today, but I'm feeling nervous.

"Don't worry, girl, I've got you covered," she says. "You go and get your man."

I laugh. "What if they're all a bunch of duds?"

"Well, what if they're not, and you meet Mr. Right this weekend?" Ellie says with a wink. She slides her chair back over to her station as a patron approaches, and soon we are inundated with people wanting to check out their entertainment for the weekend ahead.

Who knows, I think. Maybe she's right—maybe I will meet someone. I've developed a bit of a defeatist attitude towards romance over the years. It's fun in books, but I'm not sure I'll find it in real life.

Just as I am thinking that, Chris Walker approaches the circulation desk.

"Hey, Olivia," he smiles. I try not to squirm in my seat. I can feel the blush heating my cheeks.

Chris is the most handsome guy in Pine River—and also the most unavailable. He doesn't date, doesn't go to the bar on the weekend or anything. He's not even on the MeetingUp app. He's always friendly when he comes in to the library, but despite a few obvious hints that I'm single, he's never asked me out.

Maybe I'm not his type, I think. Which is too bad, because he's really, really my type. Hunky mountain man. Yum.

"Hey yourself," I say, starting to scan his books. The system beeps an error alarm. "Oh, whoops, I need your card first," I say. *Hey yourself? Forgetting his card? Who am I and what have I done with my brain?*

I've gotten tongue-tied by a pretty face before, but something in Chris's eyes is making me lose track of myself.

Chris hands over his card, holding my gaze, and I manage an awkward smile. I try not to let my eyes linger on him—try not to notice how tall he is, the way his flannel shirt sits over bulging muscles, the deep brown of his eyes.

I said I tried. I didn't say I succeeded.

"It's some weather we're having out there," Chris says. "Big blizzard coming."

"Oh, it's not supposed to be that bad, is it?" I say.

"Why, big plans?" Chris asks.

"Yes, actually," I say. I hesitate to mention it for a moment, not wanting to reveal just how single I am right before Valentine's Day. Ellie spares me the trouble.

"She's headed to a singles event in the city," she calls over her shoulder.

"Thank you, Ellie," I hiss, unable to look at Chris. My face is burning.

"River City?" Chris asks, a worried look creasing his brow.

"Yes," I say, feeling defiant. "Time for some Valentine's Day fun." I smile, but the worried look on Chris's face gets stronger.

"I'm not sure you should do that," he says. My heart pounds. For a moment, I think he is telling me not to go, not to find a date, because he is going to ask me out himself. But then he continues. "The roads are getting awful dicy. And it's going to get a lot worse before it gets better."

As if to punctuate his statement, outside we hear the roaring scrape of a snowplow going by.

"Oh, it can't be that bad. I'm sure they're already clearing it up," I say, trying to hide my disappointment. I feel ridiculous—Chris isn't interested in me. Why should I be disappointed when my little fantasies don't come to life? "Besides, I'll be fine. I just got a new car. An SUV, with four-wheel drive."

"Thank goodness," Ellie pipes up. "There weren't enough sandbags in the world to make that old compact of yours snow worthy."

"A new SUV," Chris says. "The silver Honda, out in the parking lot?" I startle, surprised that he is right.

"The very one," I say. "How did you know?" Chris laughs and shakes his head.

"Look, promise me you'll be careful tonight, alright Olivia?" he says. The worry in his eyes makes me feel warm —like he wants to protect me.

"Promise," I say. I feel my cheeks heating again. At this rate, my face is going to match my skirt soon. Bright red.

I hand him his card and his stack of items. A political thriller novel and a couple of movies. "You're all set," I tell him. "Drive safe."

"You too," he says. He smiles at me as he leaves, but he still looks worried.

Ellie and I help the rest of the patrons check out. She gives the five-minute warning over the PA, and we are swarmed with another influx of patrons.

"Phew, I think we checked out half the books in the library tonight," Ellie says. She glances at her watch. "Olivia, you'd better get going if you don't want to be late."

I look at my watch. She's right. I glance out the front window of the library and see the snow falling thick and fast.

"Be careful, okay?" Ellie says. "That storm looks serious."

"I'll be fine," I say again. "Bye! See you on Monday!"

"Have fun finding Mr. Right!" she says, with a grin. "And if you can't find him, at least find a Mr. Tonight to have some fun with, okay?"

I laugh and tell her I will. Then I put on my coat and head out of the library and into the snow.

3

———

CHRIS

The roads are already bad. I watch a truck in front of me fishtail through an intersection, narrowly avoiding collision with another vehicle. Looks like an out-of-towner—no snow tires, no chains. Neither of those are optional in Pine River, but sometimes skiers drive up here for a weekend with all of their ski equipment and none of what they really need.

I stopped off at the liquor store on my way out of town, adding a bottle of good whiskey to the weekend's entertainment. Now, I'm making my way slowly through the snow-covered streets of Pine River. The traffic is getting thinner, but there are still a few folks like me trying to get home and hunker down. Soon, it will be a ghost town, covered in a few feet of snow.

The road crews will have the snow cleared away once it stops—but there is no way that they can keep up as long as the snow keeps falling this fast. And the further I get from town, the worse the roads get.

Driving slowly gives me time to think—too much time. Olivia had looked absolutely stunning tonight. The sweater she wore showed off every one of her delicious curves. I remember the way she had blushed as we talked, how endearing her embarrassment had been.

Then I cut off that line of thinking, cursing myself. Whatever I feel for Olivia has to stay as an idle, harmless crush. She's beautiful, and as much as I want to ask her out, I can't let myself.

She deserves a better man than me.

I'm not interested in a relationship—I don't want to become a repeat performance of my parents' abuse and hatred. They say that divorce is hard on children—but the truth is that sometimes, it's worse when two people stay together. My parents never should have been married. People always told me that they loved each other, deep down, and that's why they stuck it out.

The only thing I learned from that is that love is a fairy tale, a comforting fiction that lets people sleep better at night.

I won't ask Olivia out, because I can't be the man that she deserves. There's no point—I'm not made for love. If I try to love someone, I will only end up hurting them.

I MAKE it to the state highway that leads to my cabin. I live a few miles outside of town, on my own parcel of land. It gives me plenty of space to myself—for my cabin and for the separate building where I have my workshop. It's nice and quiet, and my hammering and sawing at all hours never disturbs any neighbors. They're all too far away to hear anything.

Up ahead of me, I spot something in the ditch. A red glow of tail lights, sticking up at the wrong angle. Looks like somebody ran off the road. The car is tilted down into the ditch at a steep angle, the rear wheels not making contact with the ground.

Whoever is in that car is stuck there.

I slow down, preparing to pull over and help the hapless driver. My stomach flips when I recognize the car: a silver Honda SUV with temporary tags and no winter grunge on it.

That's Olivia's car.

My heart judders, afraid for her. Is she hurt? What had she been thinking, driving in weather like this?

I pull over and hop out of my truck, rushing towards Olivia's SUV. The snow is getting deep already, and the temperature is dropping rapidly as darkness falls.

I see Olivia, sitting in the driver's seat, staring straight ahead. At first, I think that she isn't moving—but then I realize that she is. Her chest is rising and falling rapidly. I pull open the door.

"Olivia, Olivia!" I say, trying to get her attention. She doesn't appear to be bleeding, but she keeps staring straight ahead. She is hyperventilating, her breathing coming in rapid, desperate gulps. I take one of her hands off of the steering wheel and hold it.

"Olivia, can you hear me?" I say. Slowly her head turns towards me. "Olivia, it looks like you ran your car off the road. Are you hurt?" I keep my voice level. Olivia doesn't appear to be hurt—her car hardly even looks damaged, just stuck—but she is clearly having a panic attack.

"Chris?" she says. Something in her eyes changes and I feel like she can finally see me. "What—what happened?"

"Your car is in a ditch. It looks like you ran off the road," I stroke my thumb over the back of her hand, soothing her. Her hand is cool and soft in mine.

"Oh, yeah. Yeah, I did," she says. Her eyes are wide and terrified, but she seems to be aware of what is happening at least. "I did that, didn't I?"

"And now I need you to turn off the engine and let me help you out of here," I tell her, keeping my voice gentle and even.

"Okay," she says. She's still breathing too fast.

"Olivia, I need you to take a couple of deep breaths, and tell me if you hurt anywhere." I'm terrified that she could have some injury that I can't see. If she's in shock, she might not even feel it. I realize that for a moment, when I saw her frozen in the driver's seat, I had been afraid that she was dead—and it's a selfish, stupid thought, but I was sad that I would never get the chance to take her out on a date.

But she's okay, I discover, as I help her calm down from her panic attack and check her over. She tells me that she lost control of her car and drove into the ditch. She isn't hurt, just terrified.

When I help her down out of the SUV, her legs collapse beneath her.

"Are you alright?" I say, catching her.

"I—yes, my legs just feel like jelly right now. And it's freezing c-c-cold out here." Olivia is dressed in a fashionable long wool coat—the kind that looks nice but isn't enough for a blizzard. She's also wearing heels and tights beneath her skirt.

The outfit makes her look mouthwatering. But it's not going to do her a lot of good out here in the snow.

"Let's get you out of this weather," I tell her. The blizzard is descending rapidly, approaching white-out conditions. In the darkness, the roads will be absolutely treacherous. "Can you walk?"

"I—ugh, no, I'm so shaky," she says, laughing nervously. "And my shoes keep slipping."

I scoop her up into my arms in one movement. She gives a little gasp of surprise but then snuggles in closer to my chest.

She feels so good in my arms—soft and solid, and holding her is making me think about taking her to my bed. But before I can entertain those thoughts, I have to get her out of this snow.

"I don't think I'm going to be able to get you back to town tonight," I tell her. "It's only another half a mile to my cabin, though."

"That's fine," she says. "That's—that would be nice, actually."

"Alright," I say.

"Oh, one thing," she says. "I have a bag in the back seat. Think you could grab it for me?" The look on her face is sheepish and endearing.

"My pleasure," I tell her—and I mean it. I move to the back driver-side door and carefully help her stand next to me. She clings to my jacket as I open the door and retrieve a floral bag for her. "This it?" I ask.

"That's it," she smiles. She holds out her arms, waiting for me to pick her up again. My heart skips a beat. I could get used to her reaching for me. I push the idea aside. First, I have to get both of us out of this blizzard.

The footprints I made walking from my truck have nearly been covered over by fresh snow, but I can just make out the glow of my headlights enough to find my way back to my truck. I carry Olivia in my arms to my truck and help her into the passenger side, then put her bag in the back seat of the cab. I have to shake the snow off of myself before I climb in the driver's side. It's really coming down now.

I look over at Olivia. I don't want to let her out of my sight again, especially after what just happened. I am realizing that if she got hurt, I would never forgive myself.

I pull back out onto the road and drive with white knuckles the rest of the way to my cabin.

4

OLIVIA

I glance across the truck cab towards Chris. The lights from the dashboard highlight his deep eyes, the sharpness of his jaw beneath his stubbled beard. A frown furrows his brow, and his eyes are fixed on the road ahead.

I am shaky and lightheaded in the wake of my panic attack. When I had lost control of my car, I had been so terrified that I couldn't get a handle on myself. I just kept replaying the feeling of crashing—skidding, sliding, unable to steer—over and over in my mind.

And then Chris had been there. He had talked me down and made me feel safe.

When he had lifted me into his arms, my heart had kicked hard—but from something other than panic.

I know adrenaline can make your mind fuzzy, can make you want to take risks. But the idea of being alone with Chris right now is thrilling to me—and it's a good distraction from the fear that threatens to overwhelm me again at any second. The roads have gotten worse, and I'm terrified that we will crash again. I fold my hands in my lap, wringing them together and trying to think about anything except the weather and the roads.

Part of me is regretting that I'll miss the singles event, but a bigger part of me isn't sorry at all. Even if there's no potential between me and Chris, I have a feeling that an evening with him will be more fun than any dating mixer could be.

Even if it means that I'll be spending yet another Valentine's Day alone.

"We're here," Chris says, as the truck slows to a stop. I look up. Relief washes over me. The snow whites out most of the world, but it parts just enough to give me a brief glimpse of Chris's cabin.

I knew he lived out here on the edge of town, but I've never had cause to visit him. I had thought about commissioning some work from him, just for the excuse to be with him, but even to me, that seemed a little desperate. Besides, it was out of my budget.

"It looks cozy," I say. I see a wry smile twist Chris's lips as he shuts off the engine. He has the sweetest smile. He always brightens my day when he stops by the library.

I'm going to have a lot of trouble keeping this crush of mine in check. Especially out here, all alone, snowed in together.

Chris climbs out of the truck. I unbuckle and get ready to climb out myself when my door opens. Chris lifts me into his arms.

"Good?" he asks.

"Yes," I breathe. It's incredible and intoxicating to be this close to him. I can feel the heat radiating from his body, and smell the rich cinnamon, earthy smell of him. "I should have worn boots," I say, trying to laugh off my inappropriate footwear. I feel a little silly, having him carry me—but I like it, too.

"I'm not complaining," he says with a smile, and I feel my insides turn to liquid heat. I'm breathing faster again—but it's desire, not panic, that speeds my heart now.

"Well, good," I manage, snuggling closer into his arms. Then he swings the truck door shut and the blowing snow hits us full blast. "Cold!" I shriek. I hear Chris laughing, warm and affectionate, over the roar of the wind. I tuck my head against him, shielding my face with my arm until I feel a blast of heat as we enter the cabin.

Chris sets me down gently, then flips on a light.

The cabin is charming and cozy, with a large fireplace. I look at the table that sits to my right, near the kitchen.

"Did you make this?" I ask, pointing to the table.

Chris laughs. "Yeah, I made most of my stuff. Some of it's not my best work. But it's all comfortable."

"It looks like it," I say. I notice some of the other furniture around the cabin—bookcases, a low coffee table that looks like a polished slice of log set on legs, even the end table next to the couch—they all bear the hallmarks of expert craftsmanship.

Chris smiles. "You must be hungry," he says.

"I could definitely eat," I agree. I'm starving, in fact—I didn't get a chance to grab food after work, and now that my little mishap in the snow is over I find my appetite is raging.

"I'll get something going," he says. "Let me grab my groceries out of the truck."

I glance out the window in shock. "In all this? Will you be able to find your way back inside?"

Chris laughs again. "I'll be alright. Although I could always tie a rope around my middle and let you hold one end of it if you're worried I won't come back." He means it as a joke, but it reminds me of all of the men who never did come back.

"No, it's fine," I manage with a smile. He doesn't need me dragging my baggage into this. "And thank you," I say. "I was in trouble. You saved me."

"It's my pleasure. Really," he insists. "It'll be more fun to ride out this storm with good company." I feel a blush heat my cheeks at his words, but he is out the door before I can come up with a response.

I look around the cabin some more. There's a short hallway that I assume leads to the bedroom and bathroom. The living room, kitchen, and eating area are all one big room. A couch and a comfortable-looking chair are arranged near the hearth. There is a TV off to one side, set into an entertainment center that is filled with books and small carvings. I don't want to be nosey, but I figure browsing his living room bookcase is fair.

There are dozens of small carved animals, each small enough to fit into the palm of my hand, arranged on one of the shelves. After a moment, I realize why they look so familiar. These are the carvings that Chris gives out to the kids around town. A few of them have shown them to me before, at the library. They're always so pleased and proud to have them. I pick one up and turn it over in my hands. A bear, made from a type of wood with swirling variations to its color. It's smooth, sanded to a softness that promises no splinters.

Chris comes back inside, a gusting swirl of snow following him through the door.

"These are charming," I tell him, holding up the figurine. "I've seen a few kids in town with them. They're always so proud to show them off."

Something almost shy flashes across Chris's face. "They

like them," he says. "I like making their days a little brighter."

"That's sweet of you," I say. He shrugs.

"Didn't have a lot of brightness myself, growing up. If I can make things different for them, then I figure I might as well."

I want to ask him more, but he is back out the door into the snow before I get the chance.

I replace the small bear on the shelf.

I always thought that Chris didn't date because he wasn't interested in a relationship. But the way he talked about his childhood makes me think that maybe there's something more to it than that. Maybe I'm wrong about him.

Even if I'm not, my night just got a whole lot better. I'm glad I'm missing the singles event—I'd much rather spend my weekend with Chris.

5

CHRIS

The snow is falling thick and fast as I bring in the remainder of my supplies from the truck. I hadn't meant to rush out the door so fast when Olivia asked about the figurines. But it had been all that I could do to keep from running.

Making kids smile, giving a hand up to the less fortunate kids in our community—it's important to me. But that doesn't mean I can talk about it.

And I don't know why I even brought up my own childhood. She hadn't asked—and that's something that I really don't want to talk about. I would erase it from my memory if I could. But I can't, so I hold on to those memories as a reminder of why I can't let the cycle repeat itself.

Those memories remind me of why I can't afford to love, why I can never have a family of my own. I will only pass on the terrible things my parents did to each other and to me.

At the same time, I remember something a buddy had told me once, shortly before he finally got hitched. He said that life is all about the choices we make. That if I wanted to, I could choose to be a different man than my father was. I could choose to be different from my parents. I could choose to have kids and bring them up right, in a home full of love and laughter.

I don't know if he's right. I've never really been able to believe that. But being around Olivia makes me think I might want to try.

Having her in my cabin is even harder than I expected. Seeing her in my space, knowing she's staying here, at least as long as the snow lasts—it's testing my resolve. I'm attracted to her, much more than I would like to admit. And it is taking all of my self-control to keep from making my move on her.

I am glad the storm kept her from going to that dating event, though—even though I'm sorry she crashed her car.

I shoulder my way into the cabin laden with plastic grocery sacks. Snow sprays out around me and the bags in a halo as I set them on the floor.

Olivia is curled up on my couch, her phone in her hand.

"Sorry," she says. "Just letting a few people know what happened. Don't want anyone to get worried about me when I don't show up in the city."

"Good idea," I say. "I'll start the fire, then I'll get dinner going."

"Can I help?" she asks, standing.

"No, no," I say. "You just got off work. Relax. I've got this." Besides, I like the way she looks sitting on my couch. Like she belongs here, in my space in my home.

Boy howdy. I might be more gone on this woman than I'd like to admit.

✳

"THAT WAS DELICIOUS," Olivia says. I smile, pleased to see that she has cleaned her plate. I like a woman who isn't afraid of her appetites. "Thank you." She takes a sip of her wine. The light from candles on the table between us mingles with the firelight and dances over her skin. The fire has burned down to embers, but still casts its soft glow over the room.

"Sorry you missed your event," I say, even though I'm not. "Guess you'll have to settle on having me as your valentine."

Even in the dim light, I can see the blush that colors her cheeks. "Is that so," she says. I stand and offer her my hand. She takes it and rises.

She's standing so close to me, close enough that I can smell the sweet fragrance of her shampoo. It's something soft and floral that makes me want to pull her in closer.

"I don't have chocolates," I confess. "But I did pick up a couple of movies from the library this evening. You could have your pick."

"You went to the library in a snowstorm?" she says, teasing. I feel the heat building between us as we flirt. I'm clumsy at it, out of practice, but her smile encourages me to continue. I know I shouldn't, that I should put a stop to this, but I don't want to. I want Olivia—all of her.

"I've got a crush on the cute librarian," I say. "I just wanted to see her smile."

"Ooh, I'll have to tell Ellie. Her husband will be jealous," she giggles, deliberately misunderstanding me.

I grin. "No, no, not her. The other one. Um," I snap my fingers together as if I am trying to remember her name.

"David?" Olivia says, scandalized.

I laugh, and she laughs too. Then I pull her in close to me and cup her face with my hand. I brush my thumb over her cheekbone. Her skin is so soft, and her eyes have gone wide.

"No, definitely not David," I say. "Give me a minute, I'm sure I'll think of it."

"Think hard," she whispers, sliding her hands up my chest. I'm thinking hard alright—and getting harder by the second.

"Oh, I know," I say. "Olivia. It's you."

"You have a crush on me?" she whispers.

"Mm-hmm," I reply, and pull her into a kiss. She whimpers as our lips meet, the sound sweet as honey. I can taste wine on her lips as she kisses me back. She melts into me and I pull her closer, feeling the way her soft curves press against me.

She feels even better than I dreamed, and kissing her is making me hunger for more. I slide my hand down, feeling the curve of her waist, her hip, and caressing her ass. She moans as I press her firmly against my length.

"Should we take this somewhere more comfortable?" I ask her. She looks up at me, her lips slick and pink from our kissing, and nods.

I turn away and blow out the candles. I'm planning to metaphorically burn down the cabin—not literally. Then I pull Olivia back into my arms.

I kiss her again, lifting her by her butt. She moans as she wraps her legs around me and I carry her into the bedroom.

6

———

OLIVIA

HOWEVER I HAD EXPECTED TONIGHT TO GO, THIS wasn't it.

Not that I'm complaining, mind you. Not with the way Chris is eyeing me, laid out on his bed, like he wants to eat me up. I'm thankful I wore my fancy underwear tonight—the pretty red lace bra and panty set.

Chris takes off his shirt and tosses it aside. I gasp. I knew he was fit, but I had no idea the body he has been hiding underneath all of that flannel. His muscles ripple in the dim lamplight. He crawls up the bed over me, like something predatory. He pauses at my panties. He mouths at me through the lace until the fabric is soaked inside and out and I am gasping for air.

"Please," I say. "I need you." He claims my mouth in a kiss. I spread my legs, welcoming him between my thighs. I hear the clink of his belt unbuckling, then the whoosh of denim as he slides off his jeans. But his mouth never leaves mine. He kisses like a starving man, like I am the last drink of water in the entire desert.

A part of me wants to slow down, to ask him what this

all means, where this is going. But a bigger part of me is just ready to get laid. It's been so long. And I never thought Chris would even ask me out, much less take me to his bed.

I already know that I want more from him. But I'll take this, too.

He cups my breast and runs his thumb over the edge of the lace. Then he reaches around behind me to unhook the clasp, baring me to his eyes. He drinks his fill for a long moment, then kisses me again.

"You're so gorgeous," he says, the words a breath against my lips. "I've wanted you for so long." I shiver with desire.

"Then take me," I tell him. "Take me, make me yours." He growls, sliding a hand down and cupping my sex through my panties. He slips them to one side and slides a finger into my center. I moan as he brings me to a peak with his fingers.

When I open my eyes, he is looking down at me in wonder. His pupils are wide and black with desire. I glance down between us, and I can see his manhood hanging hard and heavy between his legs.

I have a moment of doubt—Chris is big, really big, and it has been so long since I have been with anyone. But all of my fear dissolves as he slides my panties off, covering the bared skin with kisses until he is licking at my core and driving me to the crest of pleasure once again.

He kisses me again as he presses into me, joining our bodies as one. We move in sync, driving each other's pleasure higher with each thrust. I wrap my legs around him, my arms around his shoulders, needing him closer, needing him more.

"Oh, Olivia," he groans. I feel him thicken impossibly, then spill inside of me. I gasp and shudder as another wave of bliss claims me.

He holds me close as we come down from our lovemaking. I half expect him to make some excuse, to leave or kick me out, but he only tucks me in against his side and pulls the blankets up over us. He kisses my hair. I wrap my arm around him, draping it across his chest. He runs his fingers along my skin in a way that sends tingles of wanting coursing through me again—but I am too exhausted to do anything about it.

"So you mean it?" I say. "You've really got a crush on me?" I giggle at the look Chris gives me.

"Might be more than a crush," he says, his eyes gentle and dark. I feel a blush heat my cheeks and I have to glance away. I'm not sure what to make of that.

I had always thought of Chris as unattainable—but here we are, in his bed. I had written him off of my list of possibilities a long time ago. Not because I wanted to, but because I thought that I had to. I bask in the pleasure of being with him after crushing on him for so long. Tonight had started out looking like a nightmare—and turned into an absolute dream.

Chris holds me close. I feel his breathing even out as he falls asleep. I smile and sneak a glance up at him. He's even more handsome like this, with his features softened by sleep. I trace a finger over his cheekbone and fantasize about what my life might be like if I got to keep him. What it might be like to spend every night making love and falling asleep in his arms.

Not long after, I drift off to sleep, feeling safer than I can remember feeling in a long time. Here, in his arms, I am content.

7

─────

CHRIS

I WAKE AND AM MOMENTARILY CONFUSED BY THE SOFT, warm weight snuggled against my side. Then I remember last night—Olivia, panicking in the snow, then laughing in the candlelight as we ate dinner, then moaning in my arms as we made love—and I smile to myself.

Then the rest of reality sinks in and the smile fades from my face. Last night, I had let things go much farther than I planned. Too far, considering I had resolved not to let them go anywhere at all. But Olivia had broken down every barrier of resolve I had ever managed to build. She has disarmed me at every turn. Just when I think I know what to expect from her, she throws me a curveball that has me reeling in the best ways.

But last night, as I held her in my arms and made love to her, I realized she had broken through another barrier. I feel something for this woman—something I've never felt before. She makes me want to protect her, to provide for her, to be a better man for her.

I am afraid that I might be falling for her.

Which is ridiculous. Love is just a bedtime story we tell

to kids to make them think there's some hope in the world. It's a lie.

Except that what I feel for Olivia is no lie. Not at all.

I am thinking about slipping out of bed before she wakes up when I feel her stir against my side. Her fingertips dance over the skin of my chest in a way that has my body standing up and paying attention.

But I shove my desire aside. I can't risk letting Olivia get any closer. If I do, I will only hurt her. The only version of love that I have ever known was toxic—and so that's the only kind of love I could give her. She deserves better. She deserves someone who won't hurt her.

"Good morning," she says, her voice thick and fuzzy with sleep. Something warm melts inside of my chest. I recognize the feeling: it's the same one from last night, the one that had made me give in to everything that I feel for her. The one that is inching dangerously close to love.

I smile down at her, unable to help myself. She stretches, then leans in and kisses me. Her lips are soft and tender against mine, as if soothing some wound I can't quite name. She gives me a soft smile as we part.

"You sleep okay?" I ask her.

"I haven't slept that well in ages," she says, with a sheepish smile. "Must be the company."

"Must be," I say. I want to give in to the warmth of this moment, to imagine a thousand more mornings like this, stretching out into the infinity of the rest of our lives. But I can't give her that—I can't give anyone that.

It's a new feeling though—wanting to try. Thinking I might want to wake up next to this woman every day for the rest of forever.

"Well, how does coffee sound?" I ask.

"Like heaven," she replies. Then she stretches and

yawns. The sunlight pools across her skin. It's late, for it to already be light in the middle of February. But I am still reluctant to get out of bed.

"What if I make the coffee, and bring it back here?" I ask.

"You could spoil a girl like that," she answers. "But I certainly won't complain." I smile. The idea of spoiling her sounds wonderful—like it's exactly what I want to do.

I'm in uncharted territory here. The relationship patterns I know have no space for spoiling someone with affection. But I decide to risk it, to take this step and try.

For Olivia, I can try to be a better man. I can try to be the kind of man that she deserves.

"Alright then, you get cozy." I lean over and give her a peck on the lips. "I'll be back soon."

WE ENJOY our coffee in bed, talking about the snow-storms we remember over the years in Pine River.

Later, we end up making love a second time. I try to let go of my reservations, to imagine this as the start of some-thing. But there is a tugging sensation at the back of my mind, like something I've almost forgotten.

It comes crashing back to me after lunchtime.

We had made our way to the kitchen, starving, and ate cold sandwiches standing up at the counter.

After, I watch her wandering around the living room, looking at the things on my shelves. Olivia is wearing a soft-looking teeshirt and leggings that hug her curves in a way that makes me want to get her naked again. I am about to suggest just that when she pulls a thin photo album from the shelf, and my stomach turns to ice.

"Not that one," I say. But she has already opened the album.

"My goodness, you were an adorable child," she says. My pulse speeds. I cross the room in a few strides and take the photo album out of her hands.

"Don't look at that one," I say. I close the album and place it on top of the bookcase. It's a cheap move, I realize a second later. Olivia is a solid foot shorter than me. While I can reach the top of the bookcase easily, she would need to get a chair to stand on.

"Sorry," she says tentatively. "It was just baby pictures. Too many naked bathtub photos? Bad haircuts you don't want me to see?"

I look away from her. How can I ever explain it so that she will understand? It's not the pictures—it's the memories that they represent. I don't even know why I kept that photo album. I should have burned it years ago, after my mom passed. Maybe I kept it to remind myself, so that I would always remember what it was like to grow up the way that I did.

The screaming. The slammed doors, the shattering glass. The cold, alone feeling that never left. The bruises, when Dad made it past Mom and got to me.

I've heard that divorce is traumatic for kids, that some couples stay married to avoid putting their kids through that. My parents would have saved all of us a lot of trauma if they had just been able to call it quits. But right up until the end, they claimed that they loved each other.

That's what love is. It's being unable to leave something, even when it's so obviously bad for you. It's not devotion—it's blind adherence to the things that hurt us most. It's the inability to walk away, even when you should.

I can't let myself become like that. I can't bring a kid into an environment like that.

"It's nothing," I tell Olivia, but the words come out as a snarl. Then I soften. The warm, protective feelings I had felt for her this morning comes flooding back. Even if I can't love her, I can still be kind to her. "I'm the one who should say sorry," I say. "But I don't like to talk about my childhood. Not even the pictures."

"Alright," she says. But she does not come closer, does not put her arms around me and hold me. It's a feeling that I thought I had cut out and buried years ago: the need to be held.

I look out the window. "Snow's still coming down," I say. "I'll build a fire."

I busy my hands working on building the fire, and by the time it is roaring away in the hearth I am feeling a little better.

I glance over at Olivia, who is curled up on the couch.

"Want to watch one of those movies?" she suggests.

"Sure thing," I say.

HAVING Olivia curled up by my side breaks down my resolve all over again. Every time I hold her, I weaken.

We watch the movie—mostly. We make out like teenagers through a critical plot point, and by the time it ends I couldn't tell you who was supposed to be what. But I don't care.

Olivia rests her head against my chest. I toy with a lock of her hair.

"Is that why you're always giving the kids in town those little animal carvings?" she says, out of nowhere. I tense.

She lifts her head and meets my eyes, then smooths a hand over my chest, gentling me.

"Is what why," I say flatly.

"Because of your childhood. I know you apprentice kids sometimes, too—usually the ones from rough or broken homes."

"I'm just trying to make things a little better for them," I say. "Look, when I say I don't want to talk about it, I mean it." I sit up, and she moves so that she is no longer leaning against me.

"Hey," she says. "Look, that's okay. You don't have to talk about it if you don't want to." She leans in closer, trying to kiss me. But I pull away.

"I'm behind on a commission piece," I say. "I need to go do some work." I stand and go to the door, pulling on my coat and boots as fast as I can. I can feel waters pressing behind a dam, and it's going to burst if I don't get out of here, get away from Olivia.

I have to get away from her because I don't know what is on the other side of that dam.

"Chris," she says, her voice worried.

"I'll be back later," I tell her. Then I step out the door and into the snow.

8

______

OLIVIA

Despite the blazing fire in the hearth, the cabin feels cold.

One minute, Chris and I were snuggled up on the couch and I thought we were a few moments away from ending up in bed again—and the next he had fled out the door into the snow.

The snow is still falling—no longer a white-out, but still thick and fast. I can't leave, even though a part of me wants to now.

Chris clearly has some lingering issues with his childhood—and even more clearly, he is unwilling to talk about them. Or maybe he just doesn't want to talk about them to me.

I can feel the beginnings of a pattern preparing to repeat itself—one that has become all too familiar. Just when I think I've found a nice guy, and we're really connecting, he pushes me away. Or he just leaves, ghosts me.

I thought that I felt something real between Chris and me. Something that has been building, slowly, over the years of subtle flirtations. A spark that had finally caught fire. But instead, just as we were getting close, he pushed me away.

My chest aches from the rejection. I need someone to talk to about all of this, to figure out what's going on.

I pull out my phone and text my best friend Ivy. I'd sent her a text last night, letting her know where I had ended up. I'm almost surprised that she hasn't been bugging me all day for updates.

Almost as soon as the text sends, my phone rings. It's Ivy.

"You know that nobody calls anybody anymore, right?" I say, answering the call.

"Except their moms," Ivy retorts.

"Except their moms," I concede.

"I think this is too juicy for texts. So?" Ivy demands. "You spent the night at Chris's cabin? Spill, girl! Spill!"

"I—" I hesitate, a part of me not wanting to kiss and tell —but a larger part of me knowing that there's no way I can keep a secret from Ivy. She senses my hesitation like a shark scenting blood in the water.

"Olivia. I am stuck inside this stupid tiny house, all alone because John is out of town this weekend, and tomorrow is Valentine's Day. If you're off having some romantic adventure, I need to know!"

I laugh, but the sound turns to tears before I can stop it. I tell her everything—starting with crashing my car and having a panic attack, right through sleeping with Chris, and up to the point that he walked out the door.

"Oh, no," Ivy says. "Do you need me to come out there and kick his ass?"

"In this weather?" I say, managing to laugh again. Ivy always lifts my spirits. "No, no, nothing like that. I'm fine.

I'm safe. I just—I thought maybe there was something there, you know?"

"Sounds to me like there was definitely something there," Ivy says. "More than a little, amirite?" She laughs at her own joke.

"Ivy," I scold her, but there's no heat in it. "I'm just...it's the same thing as always. I think I found a nice guy, and he bails the second we get cozy."

"You'll find someone," she assures me. "And if Chris can't see what a good thing you are, then that's his problem."

"I know you found your man," I say, remembering the tumult of Ivy's romance with John. It had its rocky moments, to be sure, but it had been clear from the moment that man walked into Pine River that the two of them were meant for each other. "I'm just not sure it's in the cards for me."

"Well, if he has a lick of sense he'll come around," Ivy says. "And girl, even if he's not the one—and honestly, don't be too sure about that because you two have serious chemistry—maybe he's Mr. Valentine at least, right?"

I laugh, but the sound is hollow. "Yeah, maybe," I say. But the truth is that I want so much more from Chris. And if he isn't willing to give it, then I don't want to stick around to be strung along like some lovesick puppy.

I assure Ivy that I'm alright a few more times before we hang up. I look out the window and see that the snow has finally stopped.

I hear boots stomping outside the front door, and my stomach clenches. Chris opens the door and steps inside, snow falling from him in wispy drifts.

"Good news," he says with a smile. My heart leaps. Maybe he just needed a minute to clear his head and everything is going to be fine. But then he continues. "I convinced my buddy who owns a tow truck to come get your car. He's going to haul it out of that ditch, then he'll pick you up and take you to it."

My stomach plummets. "Oh, great," I manage. But tears sting in the corners of my eyes. I look away. A thought occurs to me. "Couldn't you give me a ride? I'm a little frightened to drive, after my crash."

"Roads should be getting cleared in town soon," Chris says. "You'll be alright." His smile is sharp around the edges, forced—not like the sunshine smiles he's had for me for as long as I can remember.

So this is Chris shutting me out. This is the door slamming behind him.

I sigh. "Fine. Whatever. I'll go pack up my things," I say. Everything I had hoped for, everything I feel for him is freezing over, hardening inside me like a block of ice. It's hard to breathe. I can't believe this is happening—and at the same time, I knew it was coming all along.

Add Chris to my long list of relationships that never even made it out of the starting gate.

9

CHRIS

I can see the pain in Olivia's eyes as I shut her out, and it makes me feel nauseous. I don't want to do this to her—but I have to. I have to cut this off before it goes any further, before my feelings for her get any more out of control.

There's only one place love leads—and it's to pain.

I see tears in her eyes as she hurries into the bathroom to pack up her overnight bag. They make my chest ache, but more than that they prove my point. By letting us get close, I've already hurt her. If I let things continue it will only get worse.

I want to go to her, to pull her into my arms and kiss her and tell her it will all be okay. But I can't. I can't even trust myself to drive her back to town. I'd turn the truck around before we got halfway there. I'd kiss her again, I'd beg her to stay.

I won't pull her into my bullshit. She deserves someone who can love her without hurting her. I only wish that person was me.

❄

I STAND OUTSIDE, watching as the town truck turns around and pulls out. The wind gusts, blowing a piercingly cold drift of snow around us. It momentarily obscures the truck. I can't even bring myself to wave goodbye to Olivia— but I can't go back inside until I see that she is safely on her way.

I stand there in the cold, watching as the truck drives away, until its red tail lights disappear into the drifting snow.

I think back to how Olivia had turned ice cold on me. I had thought that I was shutting her out—but she had closed down so tightly that I look like a leaky sieve in comparison. She had been silent for the long hour it took the tow truck to get her car and come out here to get her. I could see the thundercloud of anger hanging over her head—but whatever she was thinking, I was no longer allowed to know.

I stand there in the snow for another minute, letting the cold bite at my skin. It hurts to let her go like this. But that's what love is: pain. Olivia will move on without me.

Good, I tell myself. It's for the best.

10

___

OLIVIA

I FLIP THROUGH THE CHANNELS ON MY TELEVISION, but every single one is some sappy romantic movie. Except for one—the action movie I had just watched with Chris.

It's as if the universe is conspiring to make me feel even sadder than I already do.

I'm going to be alone on Valentine's Day—again.

I've even already texted Ellie, begging her to give me her shift at the library tomorrow afternoon, just so I will have something to do.

I had been terrified the entire time I was driving back to my apartment. The tow truck had hauled my car out of the ditch with no problem, and the paint wasn't even scratched. The driver had even helped me to clear off the snow so I could drive. The roads were mostly fine, but my head swirled with memories of the accident—and memories of Chris.

I can't help feeling like this whole situation is all my fault. I shouldn't have ever gotten so close to Chris. At the same time, though, it's as if we had both been waiting for the excuse. Our time together had felt so natural, so inevitable—until he had shut me out, cut me off, and gone completely cold.

"Maybe I'll just never understand men," I tell my cat, Simon. "Maybe I'm destined to be my own woman, forever." Simon purrs and cuddles in closer to me. "Human men, I mean." He flicks his tail noncommittally.

Still, despite how it ended, I can't let go of my time with Chris. It had felt right, being with him, like we belonged together. I can't let go of the idea that we were meant to have something more.

But if he doesn't want me, I'm not going to beg him to be with me. I just have to let go, and move on with my life.

I snap off the TV in frustration. I pull out my phone and text Ivy. I don't have to be alone after all, I realize. Not if my best friend is with me.

She texts back almost immediately.

<<I'm coming. Wine and chocolate on standby.>>

I laugh but tears well in my eyes again.

Why had I ever let myself get so close to Chris? It was like playing with fire. It's beautiful and warm, but in the end, you only get burned.

11

CHRIS

When I do go back inside my cabin, the first thing that strikes me is how empty it feels without Olivia here.

I look at the couch and remember her curled up there, the way she had looked with her legs tucked in close. I remember the warmth of her body against mine—holding her, kissing her, while we pretended to watch a movie.

I try to come up with something to do, but everywhere I look all I see are more reminders. In the kitchen, I remember the way we had laughed as we ate, our bodies still tired from lovemaking.

I pour myself a cup of coffee, but it is cold and burnt-tasting.

The bedroom is worse. I remember waking up with Olivia in my arms this morning. I remember how right it had felt to have her there, next to me.

Where had all of this gone wrong? The answer is where it always is. It had gone wrong with me. With my childhood —with the photos Olivia had found, with the way she kept bringing it up.

It had gone wrong because I can't talk about my past—and I can't trust myself not to repeat all of those patterns in the future.

I storm out of the bedroom and sit down at the table in the kitchen. I pull out my laptop, determined to focus on work. I need to enter that dining set in the competition.

But all I can think about is Olivia sitting across the table from me. The shine of wine on her lips, the glint of candlelight in her eyes.

I begin to wonder what it would be like if she had stayed. What it would be like to wake up to her every morning, to steal kisses over coffee, to snuggle up on the couch in the evenings and hear about her day. To make love to her every night.

What I want with Olivia is nothing like the relationship I saw between my parents. There's no sharp edges, no hate in the love that I feel for her. I feel no obligation to be with her, no sense of duty or bondage—only a longing to spend every day for the rest of my life waking up with her in my arms.

I stand and go over to the shelf where I keep the wooden figurines for the kids. I pick one up. It is the bear that Olivia had been looking at.

I am not the man my father was. I have chosen to live differently. I thought that refusing to fall in love, refusing to have a family of my own, was a necessary part of that. But what if I am wrong? What if my choices are the thing that matters?

I can choose to be different—I can break the cycle of my parents' relationship. Olivia made me see that. She made me see that love is something warm and protective, not a weapon used to manipulate. She makes me want to be a better man.

With her, I could build a future—maybe even a future that includes children of our own. I would work every day of my life to put a smile on their faces—and on Olivia's face, too.

A feeling like falling washes over me, plummeting and sickening. My stomach flips. I have made an enormous mistake.

I never should have sent Olivia away.

12

OLIVIA

"Okay, so we ran out of chocolate. It's not the end of the world, I promise," Ivy says. She is digging around in my kitchen, searching for a secret stash of chocolate I know isn't there.

I laugh bitterly. We had run out of chocolate—but not wine. I have been drowning my sorrows thoroughly. I'm also running out of tissues.

"I'm going to make a supply run," Ivy says.

"You can't go anywhere, you're drunk," I say. But Ivy laughs. She comes over to me, sits next to me on the couch, and strokes my hair gently.

"No, babe, you're drunk. I've had half a glass of wine," she says.

I look at the two empty wine bottles on my coffee table. "Yeesh," I say, realizing that I have apparently drunk the rest.

"Will you be okay, if I go for a minute? It's not far to the store, and I'll be in and out. I need to get something in your stomach, though, and all you've got in the fridge is tortillas and limes."

"Get tequila," I say. "Goes with the limes." I nod, as this is very wise advice I am giving my friend.

"Oookay, then," Ivy says. "Olivia, darling, you stay right here. I will be back as soon as I can."

"'Kay," I say. Ivy takes my keys with her as she leaves. "Hey, those are my car keys, what if I—" I trail off, realizing that it doesn't matter. I can't drive right now anyways. The door closes behind Ivy.

I lay down on the couch and stare up at the ceiling. This is a mistake: the world spins. "Yikes," I groan and sit back up.

Outside, darkness has fallen. The hours until Valentine's Day are ticking down rapidly, and I will be all alone.

Until Ivy gets back. I hope she gets a lot of chocolate. I need it.

My phone dings with a text from an unknown number.

<<Hey, it's chris. I...>> the message begins.

I don't even bother reading the rest of it.

"Ugh," I say, and block the number. "Not talking to you."

Then I sob—a broken, painful sound. I try to unblock the number, to bring back the text, but my fingers are too clumsy, and my tears are making the screen all blurry.

Why had Chris pushed me away? We were so good together—and the sex was *great*. I thought he was real boyfriend material—even husband material.

Apparently, I was only booty-call material. Snowstorm screwing material.

"I'm not your booty call!" I shout at my phone and fling it across the room. I collapse as another wave of tears washes over me.

I'm still sobbing when Ivy returns. I wipe away my tears with the sleeve of my sweatshirt.

"Did you get chocolate?" I ask.
"So much chocolate," she replies.
And, bless her, none of it is heart-shaped at all.

13

CHRIS

My heart pounds as I pull into the library parking lot. I realize, belatedly, that I am not even sure if Olivia will be working today.

If she isn't, then I'll just have to figure out where she is. One way or another, I have to make this up to her.

I know Olivia has spent a lot of Valentine's Days alone—I have, too. But this year, it can finally be different.

Today, I'm going to ask her to be my valentine.

Mountains of snow crowd up next to the sidewalk, still fresh from the blizzard. I make my way along the sidewalk, rehearsing my words in my head. I reach into my pocket and pull out her gift, looking it over one more time. A pale aspen bear holds a cherrywood heart in its paws. It is small enough to fit in my palm but bigger than the carvings I make for the kids. I had spent most of the night carving it, sanding it, polishing it—and practicing the words that I need to say to Olivia. Even after I finished the bear, I spent most of the night lying awake, trying to figure out just the thing to say.

I realize I am squeezing the stems of the roses in my left hand too tightly. I lift the bouquet—a dozen red roses, trite on Valentine's Day, but the florist hadn't had anything else —and smell it. The smell reminds me of Olivia's shampoo.

All that's left is to hope. The only way I can convince her I'm sorry is to show her—in front of as many people as I can manage—that I want to be with her. That I am choosing her.

I am choosing to be a better man, for her.

I take a deep breath, then open the door of the library.

14

___

OLIVIA

"Thank you," I say to Mr. Wilson, passing him his card and books. "See you next week for book club, right?" He smiles and agrees.

I don't feel as awful as I should today. My hangover had largely dissipated by noon, and although I am feeling sorry for myself, I think I managed to cry myself empty of tears yesterday. Now, I am just feeling kind of numb.

I am lost in my own head when a bouquet of red roses is laid gently on the circulation desk in front of me.

"Hi, Olivia." My heart skips a beat. I look up and see Chris standing there. I feel my eyes widen and my face flush.

"What are you doing here?" I hiss. He holds up his hands, palms out, in a pacifying gesture.

"I have to say something to you, and you're not answering my calls. Look, I need to tell you this. If you don't like it, just tell me so and I'll never bother you again. But Olivia, I realize that I made a mistake." His eyes are soft and pleading, full of that warm look he had shared with me so often this weekend—before he pushed me away.

"What do you mean?" I can feel the eyes of the patrons in the library turning to us, everyone clueing in to the drama unfolding.

"I never should have let you go. I should have asked you to stay. I was afraid—I was running from my own past. But I've realized that I get to decide what kind of man I want to be. And I've decided that I want to be the kind of man you deserve," he says.

"Chris, I—"

"Please, let me finish. Look, I never had a real example of love growing up. It was bad enough that for a long time I thought I didn't believe in love. You showed me different. You showed me what love can feel like. You showed me that I can choose to be a better man." He reaches into his pocket and pulls out a small, carved wooden bear. It holds a heart in its paws. He sets it next to the roses.

"Chris, what does all of this mean?" My heart is pounding, soaring. Everything I feel for him comes rushing back in a tidal wave of emotion. I know what I want him to say—but I am afraid that he can't say it to me.

"Olivia St. James, I love you. I'm sorry I didn't tell you sooner. Will you be my valentine?" The look on Chris's face is hope and vulnerability and joy rolled into one. My hands fly to my mouth as my eyes flood with tears.

"Do you mean it?" I say. But I can already tell that he does.

"I do. I want to spend Valentine's Day with you—and every day after, too."

"Then yes," I say. "I would love to be your valentine."

His smile glows as bright as the sun. I pick up the roses and smell them, feeling like the most special woman in the world. A few people clap, and then a wave of applause washes through the library as Chris leans over the desk and kisses me.

"One thing," I tell him, sheepish. "I'm working until five."

"No you aren't!" chimes David, appearing out of the stacks. "Get out of here. I've got this." He grins at me and I mouth a silent thank you to him.

I grab my coat and hurry around the desk. Chris proffers his arm.

"I'd like to take you on a date, if that's alright," he says. "Couldn't get a reservation this late in the game, but I did rustle up some steaks and a nice bottle of wine, and I know a little place."

"Just outside of town? Darling cabin? Has its own woodshop?" I say, with a giggle.

"That's the one," he says. Then he leans over and whispers in my ear, salacious and promising. "And it's very private."

I am glad that I am facing away from the prying eyes of the people of Pine River when I blush scarlet.

15

―――――

OLIVIA

We never do get to eat those steaks. Chris carries me through the door of his cabin like before, but this time my arms are around his neck and we are kissing before the door even closes behind us. We shed our layers and make our way to the bedroom.

Chris sits on the edge of the bed and pulls me into his lap. I gasp as I feel his hardness pressing against me. Desire burns in my blood.

"So you're my valentine, now," he says, stroking a hand over my cheek, my neck, my shoulder. "You know, I never had a valentine before." I giggle.

"Really?" I say.

"Really," he says. "Guess I was just waiting for the right woman." He pulls me into a kiss, deep and claiming. "Now, I've got one forever—or as long as you'll have me."

"Forever," I breathe, as he kisses my neck. "I love you," I tell him.

"I love you too," he says. He kisses me, then pulls back. "Say it again," he whispers.

"I love you," I say, staring into his eyes. He smiles a

smile as bright as the sun—then it shifts into something mischievous.

"The things I'm going to do to you, woman," he growls. I giggle as he kisses my neck, nuzzling me so his beard scrapes over my skin. His hands grip my hips and lift me just a little, then he turns us around and lays me out on the bed.

He explores my body with kisses, learning every inch of my skin. His beard leaves tender spots where he lingers, but I know the soreness will only fill me with joy when it brings back these memories.

He slides his fingers inside of me as his mouth reaches my center. I twist my fingers into his hair and keen as he licks at me, needing more of him. Needing all of him.

"Chris," I pant, overwrought with desire. "Please. I need you."

He moves upward then, trailing kisses over my stomach and breasts before he reaches my lips again. Then he positions himself between my legs and presses into me, opening me to him, claiming me from within.

"You're mine," he says. "I love you, and I will always love you."

"I love you, too," I gasp, as tears spring to my eyes. He kisses them away as he makes love to me—slowly, achingly, as we learn every part of one another's bodies.

I think of all of the tomorrows, of the forever stretching out before us. He is my valentine, and I am his. I cling to him as I climax, moaning his name. He follows me soon after, chanting my name like a litany prayer.

He holds me close as we come down from the heights of pleasure. He strokes my hair, pushing a sweaty lock of it off of my forehead. Then he kisses me, soft and tender. His hands are gentle as he holds me close. I sigh against his skin.

"I'm glad you said yes," he says, his voice soft in the

quiet room. It's intimate, just for the two of us. "I'm glad you're my valentine."

He looks down at me and smiles, then kisses my forehead.

"Me, too," I say, snuggling closer. "Me too."

Chris is my valentine—this year, and next year, and for every year after that.

EPILOGUE: OLIVIA
ONE YEAR LATER, ON VALENTINE'S DAY.

THERE IS A THICK LAYER OF SNOW BLANKETING PINE River, covering it in a layer of pure white that seems as though it might last forever. The ski resort has a commanding view of the mountains—and the landscape outside of the huge windows of Chez Evelyn looks like something out of a winter wonderland.

"Spring is taking its time this year," I tell Chris. We're sitting at one of the tables in the restaurant, our emptied plates having just been cleared from the table. Chris pours me another glass of wine from the bottle we're sharing. It's a special occasion, after all.

Chris smiles. "It's still February, it's got time. Besides, all of this snow reminds me of the storm that brought us together."

"It did take a blizzard to make us get our act together!" I laugh. "God, I had a crush on you for so long. This still feels surreal," I say.

Chris smiles and covers my hand with his. "Take your time getting used to it. You've got forever."

I smile again—I've been smiling so much lately that my

cheeks ache. But it's worth it. And I know there will be more days like this, too.

"So I heard your big news!" Evelyn, the head chef and owner of the restaurant, approaches our table, her hand cupped around the candle that is stuck in a mountainous slice of chocolate cake. "Congratulations, lovebirds."

"Thanks, Evelyn," I smile. She's new in town, just moved to Pine River last winter, but her restaurant has fast become a staple for both the skiing tourists and the locals. "There's nowhere else we'd rather celebrate."

She sets the cake on the table. "And I am glad to have you here. So the candle maybe says birthday more than lovebirds, but anyways, dessert is on me." She winks and grins.

I thank her. Chris and I make eye contact, then lean in and blow out the candle at the same time.

"So? Show me!" Evelyn says, holding out her hand. I catch sight of the sparkling wedding ring on her hand— Evelyn had gotten married only last year. Wedded bliss seems to be contagious in this town. I hold out my left hand, showing off the engagement ring on my finger.

"Ooh, good eye, Chris," she compliments.

"Thanks," he laughs.

"On the ring, too!" she quips, and we all laugh. She lets go of my hand and Chris takes it in his own again. "So, do you two have a date for the wedding yet?"

"Not yet," I tell her. "After all, it's only been a week since we got engaged. But we're looking at some options for this summer." Chris had taken me for a walk through town, a tour of places where the two of us had shared special memories over the past year. And then, on the steps in front of the library, he had gotten down on one knee and proposed.

Of course I said yes!

"Well, you let me know when it is and I'll get the catering arranged for you," Evelyn says.

"You don't have to—" Chris starts to say, but Evelyn cuts him off.

"Don't be silly. Besides, I have a soft spot for couples who got their start in a blizzard." She grins, blushing a little.

"You and Logan?" I ask. I knew she and her husband had a storied past, but I hadn't heard that it was a blizzard that finally brought them together, too.

"Yeah," Evelyn laughs. "Well, I'll get out of your hair. You enjoy that cake," she says with a mischievous grin.

We thank her. And then we dig into our cake.

An engagement is a special occasion, after all. Especially one being celebrated on Valentine's Day.

ABOUT THE AUTHOR

Abby loves to spin a good yarn. Even better if it's a sweet and steamy second chance romance, or a fun instalove short. And you know every story is packed full of spicy scenes, hunky heroes, and a guaranteed happily ever after!

When she's not pounding away at the keyboard, you can catch her hiking the local trails with her very own mountain man.

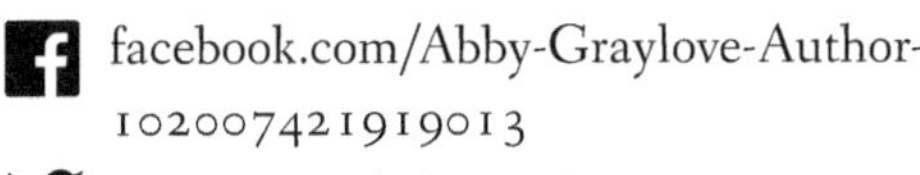 facebook.com/Abby-Graylove-Author-10200742191901 3

twitter.com/abbygraylove